Slam Dunk Series

Spider Mc Ghee and the Hoopla

Tess Eileen Kindig
Illustrated by Joe VanSeveren

CPH.
SAINT LOUIS

For my writers' group, Nancy, Laura, Laurie, Norma,
and Dandi, who always laugh at the right parts

Slam Dunk Series

Copyright © 1999 Tess Eileen Kindig
Published by Concordia Publishing House
3558 S. Jefferson Avenue, St. Louis, MO 63118-3968
Manufactured in the United States of America

Library of Congress Cataloging-in-Publication Data
Kindig, Tess Eileen.
    Spider Mcghee and the hoopla/ Tess Eileen Kindig.
        p. cm. -- (Slam dunk series)
    Summary: Mickey, sixth man for the Pinecrest Flying Eagles basketball team,
is excited when his jump shot wins the game and gets him an interview with the newspaper, but he dreams of becoming a regular starter for the team.
ISBN 0-570-07017-1
    [1.Basketball--Fiction.] I.Title.

PZ7.K5663 Sp 2000
[Fic]--dc21
                                                        99-046933

2 3 4 5 6 7 8 9 10 11   09 08 07 06 05 04 03 02 01 00

Contents

With Sprinkles
on Top

The Pinecrest Flying Eagles were about to be toast. It was the first game of the season. There was only a minute left on the clock and we were down two points.

"Outta my way, Shorty!" a Silver Maple Rocket hissed, trying to force his way past me.

I may be the smallest player on the Pinecrest A-team, but I'm fast and tricky. I held him off easy as our center, Sam Sherman, headed for the dunk.

"Go, Sam!" Pinecrest fans roared. "Go! Gooooooooo!"

Too late. Sam lost the ball. A Rocket grabbed it and let rip with a left-handed lay-up. The ball circled the rim as slow and easy as an ice skater on a lazy Sunday afternoon. It was over. We were done. Cooked. Finished. Dead meat.

Except …

It didn't go in! The ball fell over the side and hit the floor. Both teams scrambled for it. The crowd stamped its feet and whistled. The Rockets got it. Lost it. Got it back. Lost it again. My best friend, Zack Zeno, shot out of the pack, picked it, up, and pounded down the court like a torpedo.

"Dee-fense! Dee-fense!" the cheerleaders screamed.

The Rockets swarmed like red ants around Zack, but Zack was no dummy. He shot the pass to LaMar Watson of the Eagles. LaMar snatched it easy and made for the basket. Then—faster than you can say "pivot"—he passed it to me! And I hadn't seen it coming!

Everywhere I looked, red-suited Rockets swarmed. I dodged to the right, then to the left, while their guard blocked me with both arms. I started to pass the ball to Chris Jenkins on my right. Suddenly, a light bulb flashed on in my head. The Rockets expected me to go to the right again. As quick as a heartbeat, I flew to the left, and took off on a straight run to the basket.

Inside, I was a stick of dynamite ready to burst. To win this game, I knew I had to nail a jump shot. But the jump shot is my weakest thing. In fact, the jump shot is the reason I'm sixth man on the team instead of a starter. But there was no choice. Jump shot or nothing. I said a fast prayer, bent my knees, kept my eye on the target, and let it fly.

"Way to go, Mick!" Zack shouted. He was already pounding me on the back before my feet hit the floor.

The buzzer shrilled and the crowd went crazy. The Pinecrest Flying Eagles had squeaked past the Silver Maple Rockets. And I had scored the winning points. I wondered what Sam Sherman would have to say about that. Ever since kindergarten, he's called me Shrimpo. Even now that we're both on the A-team, he won't let up. Last week at practice he asked me if my uniform had to be ordered from a doll clothes company.

"Mickey, Mickey, you're so fine! You're so fine you blow my mind! Yaaaaay, Mickey!" a voice hollered.

My face turned redder than the "F" on my last math quiz. I didn't even need to look to know it was Trish Riley. She's a cheerleader for the Pinecrest Flying Eagles and my biggest fan. Everywhere I go, Trish Riley seems to go too. It's not bad enough that she lives down the street from me, but she also sits in front of me in Mrs. Clay's class at school. Don't get me wrong. There's nothing the matter with Trish Riley—that is, if you don't count one thing. She has a monster crush on me and the whole world knows it.

My mom and dad and my little sister Meggie jumped down from the bleachers and ran across the court to give me a family hug. That's what we call it when everyone hugs everyone at the same time. While I was still sandwiched between them like the white stuff in an Oreo cookie, Coach Duffy came over.

"Good job, Mickey!" he said, ruffling my hair. "We couldn't have done it without you!"

By the time I broke loose from the tangle of arms, he was already talking to Zack. But that was OK. A rush of pleasure warmed every inch of me like hot cocoa after sledding. If things kept going at this rate, I'd make starter after all. I know I should be happy to even be on the A-team. And I am happy. But I just *have* to make starter. When you want to go pro someday, like I do, you can't afford to be anything less than the best.

"Why don't you invite the team over for ice cream, Mickey?" Mom asked. "I bought a huge pail this morning at the market."

"We even got sprinkles," Meggie added.

"And chocolate sauce," my dad said, smacking his lips.

Vanilla ice cream in a plastic pail, chocolate sauce, and sprinkles may not seem like a big deal, but I could hardly believe it! First of all, my mom rarely shops at the market. She buys almost everything from this weird grocery store that gets set up every week in the basement of our church. It's called the co-op and you can shop there cheap because all the members volunteer to help. That way they can buy food for the same price the grocery store pays.

But what really amazed me about this ice cream thing, is the fact that she must have been expecting a Pinecrest victory.

"Sure, that would be great," I said. "Thanks, Mom."

I shook hands with a few Rockets, then followed my team off the court. In the locker room, Sam Sherman and the rest of the starters were already changing.

"Hey, guys," I said. "There's ice cream at my house. Everybody's invited."

Sam Sherman looked up from the bench where he was leaning over to untie his shoe. "Thanks, but no thanks, Shrimpo," he said with a snicker. "My dad's taking the starters to Pizza N' Pasta for lunch."

Pizza N' Pasta. No way could ice cream in a plastic pail compare to that. I looked over at Zack, but he was working on a knot in his shoe and didn't look up. My other friend, Luis Ramez, shrugged.

"Sorry, Mick," he said. "Sam asked me first. Next time."

"Yeah, next time," Tony and LaMar said together.

Zack still didn't say anything. I went over and sat down beside him on the bench.

"Hey," I said, low enough that nobody else could hear. "What's the matter?"

Before Zack could answer, the locker room door opened. A red-haired guy with a big camera around his neck came in. "Coach Duffy!" he called from the doorway. "Mind if I talk to one of your players?"

Coach Duffy walked over to the red-haired guy and shook hands. "Not at all, Dave. Who you interested in?"

Sam Sherman stood up and picked up his gym bag. He was trying to look casual, but anyone could see he thought the guy wanted to talk to him. The cameraman didn't even look in his direction. His eyes were darting around the room.

"I'm looking for the little guard. Number 11. There he is!" He pointed at me and grinned.

Sam Sherman grabbed his jacket and ran past the man with the camera. "Hurry up, guys!" he hollered. "My dad's out front waiting. It's the dark green Cadillac."

The door slammed behind him as the cameraman came over and sat down beside me. I knew Sam threw in the part about the Cadillac because he was mad that I got picked instead of him. Sam's dad is a lawyer in Cleveland and makes a ton of money. My dad's a welder, and Zack's dad works on the assembly line at the Ford plant making cars. Sometimes it bugs me when Sam brags about all the stuff he has that Zack and I don't. But right this minute, I was too thrilled to care about anything except the cameraman!

"Hi. I'm Dave Dawson from the *Gazette*," the guy said, whipping a pen and a small blue notebook out of his pocket. "Where did you learn to play b-ball like that?"

My face turned redder than a rope of strawberry licorice. "I-I practice a lot, I guess," I mumbled.

My first interview with a sports writer! I was going to be in the newspaper. Excitement buzzed in my bones. I grinned at Zack and shrugged. I knew I had to come up with something more exciting than what I'd just said, but I couldn't stop grinning. Zack gave up on the knot in his shoe and stood up.

"I'll see you later, Mick," he said. "I gotta go."

"No, hey, wait." I said. "You going with Sam?"

Zack shrugged. "I'll call you later," he said and walked out the door leaving me staring after him.

I couldn't believe it! My best friend was selling me out for Pizza N' Pasta. Even though they do have the best lasagna on the planet—at least everybody says they do—he had no business hanging out with Sam Sherman.

It wasn't all that long ago that Sam Sherman

stole some puppies we'd found in the church parking lot. If it hadn't been for Sam's brother, Mike, Sam would still have them, and Zack wouldn't have his dog, Piston. Mike's a great guy. He's also the best college basketball player in the state.

I turned back to the newspaper guy. He asked me how I felt when LaMar passed me the ball.

"I was a little surprised," I admitted. "I'm pretty short for the jump shot and it was down to the wire. But I was excited too. Pumped."

The guy nodded and wrote down what I said. Being interviewed was so much fun I forgot all about Zack until after I'd changed my clothes and joined my family.

"So, how many boys are coming?" Mom asked brightly. "Where's Zack? He can ride home with us. His dad must be working today."

I looked over by the pool house. Sam's father's dark green Cadillac was already gone. "Too late. Sam's dad took everybody to Pizza N' Pasta," I said, like it didn't matter. Trouble is, now that I was away from the reporter, it *did* matter. A lot.

Mom frowned. "Oh, honey, why didn't you go along with them? You didn't have to miss out because of us. We could have saved the ice cream for tonight."

I didn't want to admit that I hadn't been invited, so I let that slide by. "It's OK," I said, forcing a smile. "I've got a lot to tell you guys!"

We piled into Mom's old station wagon and I told them all about the reporter asking me what it felt like to save the game. It's a funny thing about telling a good story. You relive it as you go, and it cheers you up. By the time we turned into our bumpy gravel driveway on Arvin Avenue, I was flying high again.

"Isn't that Zack?" Mom asked suddenly. I was at the part where I told the reporter about how Mike Sherman had helped me with my jump shot.

I looked out the backseat window. It was Zack all right—looking like he'd lost his best friend in the world. I rolled down the window and stuck out my head. Mom slowed the car and stopped before she got to the garage.

"Hey, Zack," I hollered. "What are you doing home? I thought you went to Pizza N' Pasta."

Zack looked up, surprised to see us. "No. I told them I couldn't."

I broke into a grin, opened the car door, and started to hop out. "Come on in the house then," I said, "There's ice cream with our names on it."

But Zack shook his head. "I can't Mick. I've got to get home. Uh—there's stuff I gotta do."

He walked away and I closed the car door. No one said anything as Mom drove up and parked in front of the garage. It was like Zack was a magician. *Abracadabra!* He'd pulled the fun out of the day like a rabbit out of a black silk hat.

2

Project Problem

The morning newspaper hit the porch with a thud. I jumped off my chair and raced to the door.

"Mickey, don't go out there without your shoes on!" my mother shouted.

By the time I heard her, I was already reaching down to pick it up off the top step. I was so excited, I could have walked on ice. All weekend long I had been waiting for the Monday *Gazette* to see my interview. I ran into the kitchen, shoved aside my cereal bowl, and slapped the heavy newspaper down on the table. There must have been five pounds of ads before I came to the sports section.

"Yikes!" I screamed when I pulled it out of the stack.

My dog Muggsy started barking and racing around the kitchen. The rug in front of the sink twisted into a heap as he ran over it. Muggsy only came to live with us a few weeks ago. He was run over by a car and nobody thought he would live because he was the runt of the litter. But he's a real little scrapper—sort of like me. I named him after Muggsy Bogues, the shortest player in the NBA.

"What is it?" Mom asked, coming to look over my shoulder. "Oh, Mickey!" she gasped. "Look at you! You take up half the page!

She was right. The camera had caught me frozen in mid-air making the winning shot. My feet were so far off the ground, I looked like I was flying. And under the picture was a huge story with a headline that read, "Smallest Player Spins Winning Web."

"Read it! Read it!" I shouted, shoving the newspaper at Mom. No way could I read it myself. The words were running together in one big blur.

The story said that I was like a spider with so many arms and legs nobody could get past me. It talked about my defense and called me a "great find for Pinecrest." When Mom was finished, I grabbed a pair of scissors from the kitchen drawer and cut the article out. I couldn't wait to get to school and show Zack. He and his dad don't get the paper.

Zack was already on the bus when I got on. I sank down beside him on the seat and shoved the newspaper clipping in his face. "Look—it's me!" I said, not even bothering to say hi. "Is this cool, or what?"

Zack looked at the picture and frowned. "Wow. That's good, Mick. You deserved it." He handed it back to me.

I couldn't believe my ears. That's *good*? Good doesn't come close to covering it. I opened my mouth, thought of something, and shut it again. Zack probably felt left out because nobody had said anything about him.

"The story mentions you too," I assured him. "Right in the middle. It talks about how you got the ball away from the Rockets and charged the basket. Let me find it."

"That's OK," Zack said as I tried to scan the small print. "I don't care."

I folded the newspaper page. Fine, I thought. Be that way. Be jealous. I don't care. But I *did* care.

Zack and I had just had an argument a few weeks ago about the dogs Sam Sherman had found at the church. We were mad for almost two days and it had felt worse than getting booster shots. The last thing I wanted to do was start another fight.

When the bus pulled up to the front door of the school, we got off without saying anything. But we walked inside together like we always do. I didn't get it. It's not like Zack to be jealous. I didn't have time to think about it though, because right away a bunch of the guys crowded around to congratulate me.

"Nice going, Spider!" Luis Ramez, said slapping me on the back.

"Hey, Spiderman!" yelled Tony Anzaldi from clear down the hall.

My face turned redder than a fire truck, but a tingle of pleasure zipped through me.

"In your seats please, people!" our teacher, Mrs. Clay, called from the doorway of Room 16. "I have an announcement."

I slid into my desk and carefully put the newspaper clipping inside my math book to keep it from getting wrinkled. I wanted to frame it and hang it on my bedroom wall. Someday when I made the NBA, there would be *lots* of other stories. Bigger ones. Better ones. But for right now, this story was the *best* thing that ever happened to me!

Trish Riley turned around in her seat and flashed me a smile. "Hi, Mickey," she said. "You looked awesome in the paper."

"May I have your attention please?" Mrs. Clay asked. "We are about to start a very important project. It will count towards both your language arts and your history grades. So you need to listen carefully."

The whole class groaned. Trish turned around

to face the board, so I didn't have to say anything to her. The last thing I needed right now was some big project. With regular practices and weekly games, I didn't have as much spare time as I used to.

"The project is about the American Revolution. Everyone will work in groups," Mrs. Clay explained. "Each group will do one project about the war, write a report about what they have learned, and present it to the class."

She spread out a salt map, a flag, and a fort made of Popsicle sticks with little plastic soldiers glued to a board. They were the things people had made last year. My mind did a fast pivot. This Saturday we were playing the Red Oak Rangers. Luis Ramez told me they're pretty hot. His cousin lives by Red Oak Park and knows a lot of their players.

"Group one will be Mickey, Trish, Zack, and Sam," Mrs. Clay was saying.

I snapped to attention. Trish whipped around in her chair and mouthed the word "Sam" at me. She made a face. My feelings exactly. No way could Zack and I work in a group with Sam Sherman. Even Trish was a thousand times better than Sam Sherman.

When the bell rang for lunch, I marched over to Mrs. Clay before I chickened out. "Excuse me," I said politely. "Does Sam Sherman have to be in our group? He—uh—he—I mean we ..."

Mrs. Clay folded her arms and looked at me. I ran my hand over the stick up hair on the top of my head, and shifted my weight to the other foot.

"I know there have been some problems between you boys, Mickey," she said, staring at me from behind her glasses. "That's why I chose you to work together. I'm hoping you can learn about teamwork, and maybe even get to be friends."

A million words rushed to my mouth to explain why there was no way Sam Sherman and Mickey—make that *Spider*—McGhee would ever be friends. But I just nodded miserably and slunk off to the lunchroom. Mrs. Clay didn't get it. Sam Sherman has been making my life miserable for four years already. Even if I wanted to be friends with him—which I didn't—he didn't want to be friends with me.

I grabbed my usual seat next to Zack, but I didn't open my lunch bag. After getting stuck on a project with Sam Sherman, I didn't feel much in the mood for peanut butter and grape jelly. Zack looked up and said hi. But that's all. He was peeling an orange like it was a science experiment.

"I tried to talk to Mrs. Clay about Sam," I told him. "She says we need to learn teamwork or something. Man, this is going to be terrible!"

Zack shrugged. "It doesn't matter."

I stared at him like he'd grown antlers. This was not my old buddy Zack talking. This had to be some guy *pretending* to be Zack. "Are you crazy?" I squawked. "You know how bossy he was when we were practicing for basketball tryouts."

Zack shrugged again and started piling his orange peels in a stack. "We're already playing with him on the team," he said. "What's the big deal?"

I didn't know how to answer. Mostly because I still couldn't believe what I was hearing. Were Sam and Zack friends and I didn't know about it? They were both starters, after all. And I wasn't. But Zack didn't go to Pizza n' Pasta with Sam and the rest of the starters after the game. If they were friends, he'd have gone. Sam's dad was paying, so it wasn't a matter of his not having any money. This was getting very strange!

I put my hand over Zack's stack of orange peels so he couldn't add any more. "What's the matter with you?" I demanded. "You've been acting weird."

Zack shoved my hand away from his tower. It tipped over and scattered across the gray tabletop. "Nothing's wrong with me," he snapped. "Nothing *you* can do anything about anyway."

Before I could take that in, Sam Sherman walked over to our table. He was carrying a carton of chocolate milk in one hand and a straw in the other. "Hey, Zack," he said, as though I weren't sitting there. "Our group meets tonight. My house at 4:00." He stuck out his straw like a pointer and added, "Be there."

"Hey, what about me?" I called as he started to walk away. "I'm in your group too, you know. So is Trish Riley."

Sam wheeled around and started to laugh. "Sure, Shrimpo," he said. "I meant you too." He walked over to join his friends at their table near the wall. They all looked at me and laughed.

I could feel my face getting hot. The minute I get even the slightest bit embarrassed I turn red as a live coal. I jammed my uneaten sandwich back into the bag and stood up. "You coming?" I asked Zack. "I'm going outside."

Zack shook his head no. "I'll catch up with you later," he said.

"OK." I took a few long sips of my milk and tossed the empty carton into the trash. I didn't know if I was madder at Sam for making fun of me, or at Zack for acting so weird.

Out on the playground, Trish and the other cheerleaders were practicing cheers. They were hollering something about opening up the barn door and kicking out the hay. What that has to do with basketball is anybody's guess.

I didn't feel like shooting hoops, so I walked over by the fence and slumped down on a bench facing the road. An old blue van pulled into a space in front of the school. A tall guy with coal black hair and a black moustache got out. It was Zack's father.

Mr. Zeno never came to school in the middle of the day. Whenever we had plays or awards, he could never come because he always had to work. An uneasy feeling crept along under my skin like a snake. Slowly, I got up and walked down the length of fence to where the path leads to the front door of the building. Mr. Zeno turned up the walk and headed toward me. He was wearing clean jeans and his orange bowling team jacket.

"Hi, Mr. Zeno!" I called. "You looking for Zack?"

He waved, but didn't say anything until he got right by the fence. "Hi, Mickey. No, I have an appointment inside." He looked at his watch. "I'm running late too."

"I'll tell Zack you were here," I said as he walked by me.

That spun him around. "NO!" he cried. "I mean, I wish you wouldn't, Mick."

I waited for him to say something else, but he

didn't. So I said the only thing I *could* say which was, "Yes, sir. I mean, I won't, sir."

He thanked me and pulled open the door of the building. I watched him go in and head down the hall to the office. Behind him the door slowly closed. As I watched it, the uneasy feeling coiled around the pit of my stomach and squeezed hard. If Mr. Zeno was at school in the middle of a work-day, it could only mean one thing.

My best friend was in big trouble.

3

A Letter from the Universe

"OK, guys, here's the plan," Sam Sherman announced at the project meeting. "We're going to do a play."

"A play!" Before I knew it, the words flew out of my mouth. "Don't we at least get to vote? I think we should vote. I vote no."

I looked at Zack for back up, but he just sat there staring at the design in the rug. I had been thinking more along the lines of a salt map. The last thing I wanted to do was dress up in funny clothes and make a fool out of myself.

"But, Mickey, a play could be fun," Trish said eagerly. She turned to Sam. "As long as I get to be Betsy Ross."

"Sure, sure," Sam told her. He reminded me of somebody trying to shoo away a fly.

"I want to wear one of those little white caps with a lace ruffle," Trish continued. "And a shawl. I must have a shawl. Oh, and I need one of those round hoop things to put the flag in while I'm sewing it. OK?"

Sam ignored her. He was standing in front of the marble fireplace in his living room checking things off a list. "I will play the part of General Washington," he said. "Zack, you can be Paul Revere and ..."

"I *want* one of those hoop things, Sam," Trish interrupted. "And a shawl. Why aren't you listening to me?" She jumped up off the fancy velvet couch and grabbed his notebook. "This play isn't just yours, you know. And I definitely want lines. I'm not going to just sit there on stage, sewing the whole time."

Sam took back his notebook. "You can have whatever you want," he told her. "Just sit down and let me finish."

"Shrimpo, you're a soldier," he said to me.

"What soldier?" I asked.

"Any soldier," he answered.

Anger rose in my chest. Everyone had a name in the play except me. Everyone, except me, got to be someone famous. As usual, Sam Sherman was running the show. Only this time I wasn't going to let him get away with it.

"I don't want to be a soldier," I said, crossing my arms over my chest. Even as I said it, I knew it wasn't true. It would be cool to be a soldier, *if* I got to have one of those cow horns the Revolutionary War guys used to keep their gunpowder in. I could scratch my name on it just like they did in the olden days.

Trish jumped up off the couch again. "I think Mickey should be Ethan Allen with his Green Mountain Boys. Ethan Allen was a soldier, only famous. Mickey should definitely be somebody famous." She smiled at me and tugged on the brim of her Cleveland Indians baseball cap.

Whenever Trish starts tugging on one of those caps she always wears, it's usually a sign for me to make tracks. But I was glad to have somebody agree with me.

Sam shrugged. "Whatever," he said, flipping the page in his notebook. "Anyway, I talked to Mrs. Clay and she said that if we do a play, we don't have to do a report. The play *is* the report. The way I see it is, Trish, you can do the costumes and I'll write the script. Zack, you can make up a program. My dad will make copies for us at his office. Mickey, you're on props."

I didn't like being told what to do, but props sounded easy. Especially compared to writing a script. The anger shifted and settled in my chest like cereal in a box. Sam would be pounding computer keys, and I'd be sharpening my b-ball skills. What could be better than that?

After the meeting, Zack and I walked out the big, heavy wooden door of Sam's house together.

A light snow made the street look like a Christmas card. Sam lives in this area of big, old houses that rich people are fixing up. His is red brick with a huge pointed stained glass window on the side. When you're standing in the front hall you can see it on the landing of the stairs. It glows red, blue, and yellow just like the stained glass windows at church.

"So, what do you think about the play?" I asked Zack as we walked down the long driveway together. I was glad the snow had kept us from riding our bikes. Walking gave us a chance to talk.

Zack turned up the collar on his jacket and stuffed his hands in his pockets. "It's OK," he said. "I don't mind."

We walked the rest of the way down the driveway without talking. Trish's mom had come to pick her up and had offered us a ride home. I almost wished now that I had said yes. It felt weird trying to talk to Zack about a problem he didn't know I knew he had. It was especially hard, since I couldn't tell him I'd seen his dad at school.

As we turned onto the sidewalk, I picked up a handful of snow and tossed it at Zack. He brushed it off the front pocket of his old green jacket. I could see that the sleeves were getting a little short. His long skinny wrists stuck out from under the elastic like two sticks.

"By tomorrow there should be enough of this stuff for us to make a fort," I said.

"Yeah," he answered. But I could tell he didn't care about snow forts.

We walked to the corner and turned right. I'd been hoping that once we got off by ourselves, he'd at least give me an opening. He sure wasn't making it easy.

"Did you hear Coach Duffy say he was going to talk to us about baseball passes?" I asked as we crossed the street. "I don't even know what that is. Do you?"

Zack shrugged. "It's for when you get a rebound. You toss the ball with one hand kind of like a baseball. It's no big mystery."

His voice was flat, but there was a sting to the words. I felt the anger that had settled in my chest rise again. I had *had* it with this stuff. Zack had been acting weird for three whole days. It was time for a straight answer. I stopped in my tracks on the sidewalk and crossed my arms over my chest. "OK, Zack," I demanded. "What's going on?"

Zack started to say "nothing," but I held up my hand to stop him. "No way," I said. "Something's wrong and I'm not moving until I find out what it is."

Zack shuffled his feet in the snow for a second,

and then started walking toward Wooster Street. "I don't want to talk about it, Mick. I'm not even sure what's going to happen yet."

"Are you in some kind of trouble?" I asked, running a little to catch up. "Because if you are, you can tell me and I'll help you." I meant it too. If Zack had a problem, *I* had a problem. That's what being best friends is all about.

We walked down Wooster Street past the hardware store to the traffic light.

Finally Zack said, "I know you would, Mick. But I just can't talk about it right now. OK?"

For a second I didn't answer. It kind of bugged me that he would keep a secret from me. If I had a problem, I would tell *him*. But there wasn't any choice. I had to say "OK." As much as I hated it, Zack had the right to keep his problems private if he wanted. But what he couldn't do, was stop me from praying for him. I would pray like crazy until everything was all right again.

"Will you at least tell me sometime?" I asked.

Zack nodded. "You'll find out sooner or later, Mick. I promise. So will everybody else."

I didn't know what to say to that, so I didn't say anything. My mind flooded with thoughts about what could be wrong. But none of them made any sense. We waited for the light to change and watched the stream of cars go by.

"Hey," Zack said, suddenly brightening. "I just thought of something. I have one of those feather pens left over from my cousin's wedding. You can use it as a prop. Maybe George Washington could sign something with it. It's really a ballpoint, but I don't think that would matter. Do you?"

"No, it would be cool," I said. "Yeah, we'll use that for sure."

I looked up at the clock on the bank as we crossed Wooster Street. It was only 4:30. "Want to come over for a while and show me how to do a baseball pass?" I asked. "My mom could drive you home."

Zack grinned. "We can't play basketball in the snow, you dork," he said.

I laughed and smacked my forehead with the palm of my hand. I was so glad to hear Zack acting normal, I'd forgotten all about the snow.

"I'll come over anyway," he offered. "Maybe we could hunt around for props."

"Or I could help you do a program," I agreed.

We turned onto Arvin Avenue, tossing snow at each other and sliding on the icy spots on the sidewalk. At my house, the kitchen light cast a yellow glow through the late afternoon darkness. It looked nice—all warm and cozy like a house on TV.

We went in the side door and up the steps to

the kitchen. I could smell spaghetti sauce simmering on the stove. As I pushed open the kitchen door, Muggsy and Meggie nearly knocked us over.

"Mickey, you got a letter!" Meggie hollered. "A real one. The mailman brought it and everything. Mama says it's from the universe."

Zack howled. "The *universe*? Gee, Mickey, you must be some important guy!"

I scratched Muggsy's ears and fought my way through the door. "Where is it?" I asked her.

Meggie ran to the table and brought back a long white envelope. She shoved it in my hand and glared at Zack.

"It is too from the universe," she said. "The state universe. My Mama said so."

I looked down at the address in the upper corner of the envelope and let out a yell. Muggsy barked and ripped through the kitchen, leaving the rug by the sink in a heap. Meggie was almost right. The letter was from the State University.

The State University *basketball* team.

The Sandpaper Kid

My hands were shaking as I opened the letter.

"Gee, Mickey, do you think maybe they heard about the Silver Maple game?" Zack asked. "Wow! They might want you to come play for them when you get out of high school."

"No way," I replied. "It's too early for that. It's two more years before we even get to middle school."

I couldn't help but wonder though. Maybe Zack was right. That had been a pretty great story in the paper. I could sure see where it might get people talking.

Some green cardboard things fell out of the envelope onto the floor. I let them go and unfolded the letter. It was written on university paper and signed by the coach. My eyes zoomed over the lines of small print.

"Oh, man!" I screamed before I even finished it. "Oh, *man!*"

"Mickey, what's the matter?" Mom cried, running up the basement steps. "Is something wrong?"

I shoved the letter in her hands. "No!" I hollered. "Something's right! Something's so right I can't believe it. Say yes, Mom! Please, say yes!"

"What is it?" Zack asked. "Are they recruiting you?" His eyes were as big and round as two quarters.

They weren't recruiting me exactly—at least not to play ball on their team. But they *were* asking me to be a ball boy at their game the week before Thanksgiving.

Already, I could see myself down on the court chasing the out-of-bounds balls and tossing them back to the players. The gymnasium would be packed. The band would be playing. And before the game I would be out on the floor shooting a zillion baskets.

Zack reached down and picked up the green things that had fallen out of the envelope. "Look, Mick," he said. "Tickets. They sent you four free tickets to the game."

"It won't even cost anything, Mom!" I begged, grabbing the tickets and waving them in front of her face. "Please say we can go. I want to be a ball boy more than anything!"

Meggie grabbed the hem of Mom's sweatshirt and started tugging. "I wanna be a ball boy too!"

she whined. "I wanna do what Mickey does."

"A ball boy!" Zack exclaimed. "Oh, man, Mickey! Wow!"

"You could come with us," I said to Zack. "There are four tickets and I won't need one to get in. Can Zack come too, Mom? Can he?" I asked.

Mom laughed and backed away from us. "We'll have to talk it over with Dad, but I think we can probably work it out," she said. "Of course, Zack can come." She pried Meggie's fingers lose from her shirt. "As for you, Miss Meg, you'll be too busy eating hot dogs to be a ball boy."

"Yay, hot dogs!" Meggie cried. She ran off to the living room to watch cartoons with Muggsy yipping at her heels.

"You know, Mickey, you have Mike Sherman to thank for this," Mom said, as she read the letter. "It says here that he told the coach about you."

I had been so excited to be asked to be a ball boy, I'd never read past the first few lines. I couldn't believe it. Mike Sherman played center and was the star of the team. I'd only met him a few weeks ago when he'd helped me with my jump shot at the park. Now he'd gone and done something this great for me!

"Wow!" I breathed. "Wait till Dad hears this!"

My Dad is almost as big of a basketball freak as

I am. The second we heard his truck pull in the driveway, Zack and I clattered down the steps to the side door.

"What's this, the welcoming committee?" he asked when he pushed open the door.

I told him the news and he let out a howl so loud it made Muggsy howl too. "Can we go? Are you kidding?" he shouted. "Mickey, we'd walk if we had to!"

It wasn't until that night when I was lying in my bed looking out the window at the streetlight, that I remembered. Zack had never said he would come with us. Some of my excitement slipped away as I thought about how sad Zack seemed now.

There was only one thing to do for him. I folded my hands over my blanket and looked up at the ceiling.

Hi, God, it's me, Mickey. I'm worried about Zack. He feels really bad, and I don't know how to help him. I don't even know what's wrong with him. But I know You do. I also know You love him and his dad a lot, and will be with them through whatever it is. But do You think maybe You could show me how to help them too? Zack's my best friend and I can't stand not doing something. Thanks God. I knew I could count on You.

I rolled over and closed my eyes. "Amen,"

I whispered.

The next day we had practice right after school. The snow was gone, so Zack and I pulled on ski hats and rode our bikes over to Pinecrest Park. By the time we stamped into the locker room our faces were red from the cold wind.

"Hey, Mick!" Jack Miller called. "Is it true what I heard about you being a ball boy for a State game?" Jack's a bench-sitter on the team. I don't know him too well.

I looked over to the lockers against the wall. Sam Sherman was lacing his shoes. Part of me wanted to say "yes" loud enough for him to hear. But another part didn't want to risk having him spoil the whole thing. I shrugged and sort of grinned.

"Wow," Jack said. "Lucky you!"

Lucky me all right. Lucky to get to do it. And lucky that Sam Sherman didn't seem to have heard. I changed my clothes fast and headed out on the court before he could look up and call me "Shrimpo."

Zack and I practiced our free throws until Coach Duffy blew his whistle. "OK, guys, listen up," Coach said as the whole team gathered around him. "I'm not going to sugarcoat this. The Red Oak team is good. Make that *better* than good. They may well be the strongest team in town. We've got a real fight on our hands. But I think we can do it."

I looked over at Zack. He was staring down at the floor.

"Zack! You listening?" Coach asked.

Zack's head snapped up. "Yes, sir," he said. "We have to give it all we've got."

Coach nodded and went on with his pep talk. I listened, but my eyes were on Zack. I knew he hadn't heard a word. The only reason he knew it was a pep talk is because Coach Duffy always gives us a pep talk before practice.

After warm-ups, Coach showed us the baseball pass. "This is your best pass when you need to cover a long distance," he explained. He brought the ball back behind his shoulder and whipped his throwing arm forward. The ball came hurtling toward Zack. It hit the floor. Zack hadn't been ready.

"What's the matter with you, Zeno?" Sam scoffed.

Zack looked at the ground and muttered, "Sorry."

"No problem," Coach Duffy said. "But you aren't really with us today, Zack, and we need you. Saturday's game is not going to be a picnic in the park. I need to know I can count on every single one of you. Got that?"

Zack nodded miserably. I don't think I'd ever seen him so embarrassed. That is normally my department.

After practice we hurried into the locker room. I knew Zack just wanted to change and head for home. He was in no mood to talk to anybody, and neither was I. But Sam Sherman was in no hurry to get home. He came over and handed me a piece of notebook paper.

"Here," he said. "The script is done for the play. These are the things we need for props. Do you have any of this stuff?"

I took the paper. My eyes roamed over a column as long as a greedy kid's Christmas list. Finally I hit on the one thing I had. "Yeah," I said. "I've got the feather pen."

"It's called a *quill* pen," Sam corrected me.

"Quill. Feather. Whatever," I said. "Either way, I've got it."

"Where did you get it?" he demanded.

I looked over at Zack. "I gave it to him," Zack replied. "It's left over from my cousin's wedding."

Sam laughed. "We can't use that. They didn't even invent pens like that back then."

I felt stupid. I knew they didn't really have ballpoint pens in the olden days. So did Zack. We just didn't think we needed to get so picky. The important thing was that it *looked* like a quill pen. Before I could say that though, Zack jumped in. "Mick's chopping the pen part off," he said. "Don't worry about it."

Sam nodded and I grinned at Zack. But I stopped grinning when I looked down at the list again. Almost everything on it was something that had to be made. Swords. Hatchets. Muskets. No way could we get real stuff like that.

I opened my mouth to say it wasn't fair for me to have make that many things by myself, but Sam jumped in first.

"By the way, McGhee, it looks like I'll see you at the State game," he said. "I'm a ball boy too. I get to do *every* home game this season."

The look on my face must have been what he was waiting for. He laughed, yanked a towel from around his neck and pretended to snap me with it.

At least I *think* he pretended. I didn't stick around long enough to find out for sure. I grabbed my gym bag and my jacket, and banged out of the locker room. Leave it to Sam to wipe the shine off the day, I thought as I walked down the hall. He was just like sandpaper. *Scritch. Scratch.*

5

A Maze of Blue

"I'm calling a project meeting," I announced as soon as I walked into Mrs. Clay's class. "After school. My house." I pointed my finger at Sam and said, "Be there."

Sam laughed. He knew I was imitating him. "No can do, Shrimpo," he said. "I have to get my hair cut and then my family's going out to dinner."

"I'll be there, Mickey," Trish offered.

"Me too," agreed Zack.

I slumped in my seat and stared at the bulletin board already decorated with Thanksgiving turkeys. I should have known Sam wouldn't come. He knew why I was calling a special meeting. I needed help making all those props.

Mrs. Clay had been in the hall talking to the principal. Now she came into the room and told everyone to take a seat. "I need to be gone for awhile this morning," she said. "Miss Winders will take my place. I want you all to work on your projects. You can break up into groups and talk quietly. Zack, will you come with me, please?"

My mouth dropped open as Zack stood up. For a second a confused look came over his face. Then he blinked hard like he might burst into tears. Nobody said a word as he walked out of the door with Mrs. Clay's arm around his shoulder. That could mean only one thing. I was wrong. Zack wasn't in trouble. He had family problems.

It was after 10:00 before Mrs. Clay came back. She started right in on science like nothing had happened. At 10:30, there was no sign of Zack. 11:15. No Zack. 11:30. *Still* no Zack.

At noon, when the bell rang for lunch, I grabbed my brown sack from my locker and headed to the lunchroom with Tony and Luis. Just as we turned out of our hall, we saw him coming out of the counselor's office.

"Zack!" I called, ducking out of line. Mrs. Clay didn't even try to stop me. "Are you OK?" I asked him.

"No," he answered.

The word sent a buzz through my bones. It felt like the shock you get when you turn on the TV after you've walked across the carpet in your socks. "No?" I echoed.

Zack pulled me over by the window. "I might as well tell you, Mick," he said in a low voice. "I'm going to be leaving pretty soon."

Outside, soft flakes powdered the pine trees in front of the school. A blue car drove slowly down the street. The mailman, carrying a big stack of letters, turned up the path to the building. It was weird. The whole world was as scrambled as a pan of eggs, and yet somehow it still looked normal outside.

"What do you mean, leaving? I don't get it." I said.

Zack answered, "I mean that I have to go to Chicago. My dad got laid off at the plant. I—I don't even get to be with him, Mick." His chin trembled. Two big tears rolled out of his eyes and dripped onto his shirt.

"He got a job with the railroad until he gets called back at the plant in April. But he has to go to Minnesota for the rest of the winter, and I have to go to my aunt and uncle's house. I don't even know them, Mick!"

I looked around. Kids were rushing past us, laughing. The hall smelled like tacos.

"When do you leave?" I asked. My voice sounded hoarse.

"The Sunday after Thanksgiving. I'm scared, Mick."

I swallowed hard. I didn't know what to do. Trish came by and started to say something. When she saw us, she changed her mind and walked on.

"We'll think of something, buddy," I said finally. "We will. We *always* think of something. Don't we?"

He nodded. For a second, a hopeful look played on his face. Then, almost right away, it disappeared. "I think this might be a little different," he said.

True. Compared to having to go live with somebody you didn't even know, making the team and finding lost puppies was small stuff.

Things must be pretty bad for Zack's dad to send him away. It scared me even to think about being sent away from my parents.

After school, the project group met at my house like we had planned. Since he wouldn't be leaving until after the play, Zack came too. We agreed not to talk about Chicago in front of Trish. Zack wasn't ready for everybody to know yet. To be honest, it felt sort of good to act normal, even if it was only pretend normal.

"The first thing we have to do is start making props," I said when everybody was sitting around the big metal table in my basement. "There's way too much here for one person. What should we start with?"

Trish looked over the list. "Oh, goody! I get a round thing to put the flag in while I sew it!" she squealed. "My grandma has one I can use. And I have a big flag at home."

"Maybe we ought to make a rifle for me to be Ethan Allen," I said.

"Cool," Zack agreed. He seemed better now that we were away from school, but I knew it was mostly because of Trish. "What will we make it from?"

I got up and yanked a huge piece of cardboard out from behind a ladder against the wall. "This." I dragged it over to the table. "The people next door got a new fridge."

Trish ignored the cardboard. She had spotted the shelf of boxes where my mom keeps her craft stuff. She jumped up and ran over to check it out. "May we use any of these things, Mickey?" she asked, pulling out a huge roll of satin ribbon. "This is the prettiest shade of blue I have ever seen. What do you think we could do with it?"

Zack and I didn't answer. We were busy studying Ethan Allen's rifle in our history book. It was so long it would probably wind up being taller than I was.

"Hmmmm." Trish puckered up her forehead and frowned at the ribbon. "We just have to use this! Wait—I know! We could tie it on the ends of your pigtails and make pretty bows. You guys have to have pigtails. All the men had them back then."

Zack and I groaned. History or no history, we weren't wearing hair ribbons. "Forget that," Zack told her. "Come help us draw the rifle. You're the best artist."

Trish set the ribbon in the laundry basket next to the shelf and came over to the table. "I guess I am," she agreed. "But you'll have to move out of my way if you want me to do a good job. I need room to work."

Zack and I got up and let her draw. I went over to the shelf of craft stuff and started rooting around in the biggest box. I was looking for this basket we'd had on the dining room table last Thanksgiving. It was supposed to be a horn of plenty, but it was shaped exactly like a gunpowder horn.

"Aha!" I cried, pulling it out from under a pile of fake fruit. I held it across my chest. "What do you think?" I asked Zack.

"Cool," he said. "All we need is a piece of wood to stop up the opening and a string to tie it to." He actually sounded a little interested. But I knew he wasn't. Not really. What did gunpowder horns matter when you were being sent away from home?

We went over to my dad's workbench and started looking for wood. Pretty soon Meggie came clattering downstairs.

"Whatcha doin'?" she asked, dragging a chair over to the workbench. "Can I help?"

"No!" I snapped. "Go watch cartoons. We're busy down here."

I knew I was being mean, but I felt like I was going to explode. Acting normal when everything's awful is like trying to pretend there's not an earthquake when the whole house is shaking.

Meggie stuck out her lip and pouted. "I want to make something!" she demanded.

"Then make something," I said. "But do it upstairs, OK?"

Meggie left the chair by the workbench and wandered around the basement. First she watched Trish draw. Then she tried to build a tower out of odd-shaped chunks of wood. When they crashed on the concrete floor she went over to the craft shelf. The next time I looked up from my work, she was back upstairs again.

"Look!" I said to Zack, pulling out a long, brown lace from a work boot. It was in a box with a bunch of stiff old paintbrushes. "We can tie this on the horn. Then maybe Mom would let us use one of these brushes to paint the basket a darker brown."

Zack stuck one end of the lace into the weave of the basket on the wide end, while I did the pointed end.

"Mick-keeeeeeee!" Meggie called from upstairs. "There's a boy with loom-in-num-in-num to see you!"

Trish looked up from her drawing and giggled. "What loom-in-num-in-num?"

"Aluminum," I answered. Who would be at my house with aluminum? I looked at Zack and shrugged.

"I'll finish up while you're gone," Zack said.

I ran up the stairs. Mom wasn't in the kitchen and neither was Meggie. I could feel a draft from the front door. Somebody really was waiting for me in the doorway. Quickly I went around the basement door to the living room.

Whap! My legs crashed into something.

"Owwwww!" I yelled. My funny bone banged against the doorjamb as I hit the floor. Sizzles of pain like a Fourth of July sparkler shot through my arm.

I looked around and gasped. Yards of blue satin ribbon crisscrossed crazily back and forth all over the living room. Ribbon connected the doorknob with the leg of the coffee table. The leg of the coffee table with the window lock. The window lock with the stair post. The stair post with ... It would have been an awesome maze—except for one thing. I was the rat who'd gotten caught in it!

"Moooooooooom!" I yelled.

Meggie crawled over to me under the weave of blue ribbon. "Don't be mad, Mickey," she said. "I made a present. I tied up the whole living room like a big present.""Yeah, Mickey, don't be mad. Where's your sense of humor?" a voice asked from the doorway. I looked over to see Sam Sherman standing by the door laughing like crazy.

"Look. I brought you something," he said. He held out two boxes of aluminum foil. "I thought you could use it to make swords."

I stood up, carefully stepping over the booby-trap ribbons. I had to lift my legs practically to my chin to do it. Step. Lift. Step. Lift. All the way to the door. "Thanks," I replied as I took the boxes. "These are great. I'll see you tomorrow." I hoped I sounded less goofy than I felt. I knew my face was redder than the stripes on a candy cane.

Sam opened the door and walked out on the porch. At the steps he turned around.

"Hey, Shrimpo," he said. "Tell Zeno I'm sorry about whatever's going on."

I couldn't believe my ears. Sam Sherman sorry about someone else's problems? I wanted to look up and see if the sky were falling.

Halfway down the walk, he turned around again. "By the way," he called, "that was an a-*mazing* show you just put on! Wait till I tell the guys!"

Now *that* was more like it.

6

A Whopper Doozy of a Problem

It was halftime. The Pinecrest Flying Eagles were down by six against the Red Oak Rangers. I leaned against the wall and took a swig from my water bottle. I'd scored four points and made two assists, but I was off my game. All I could think about was Zack leaving. In less than two weeks he would be in Chicago.

"Guys! Over here! Now!" Coach Duffy barked. His face was as red as the cherries in a can of fruit cocktail.

I set down my water bottle and joined the team in a huddle. Already I could hear what was coming. He was mad because we weren't working hard enough.

"OK, listen up!" Coach snapped, looking at each of us, one by one. "We can still nail this game. But to do it, we're going to have to get tougher on defense. Mickey and Zack, I want you to pull out the stops. Sam, you're going to have to focus out there. You can't be watching the cheerleaders."

A laugh bubbled up inside me. I swallowed it before it erupted. Sam scowled.

"You're holding back, guys," Coach continued. "All of you. We can't afford it. Red Oak has a big advantage. In case you haven't noticed, their guys are bigger than most of you. But size doesn't mean everything." His gaze fell on me for a half a second. "What matters is how well you play the game. And you guys play a great game when you put your minds to it!"

"Yeah," LaMar agreed. "We've just gotta go out there and show 'em what we can do."

"Right!" the rest of us agreed.

Coach grinned. "What did you say?" he asked, cupping his ear with one hand. "I can't *hear* you."

"Right!" we roared.

I yelled as loud as anyone, but the truth is, I wasn't feeling it. I loped out onto the court beside Zack, wishing I could just go home. It was no surprise when Red Oak took control of the ball right away. I tried to block their guy. So did Zack and Tony, but he was as slithery as a snake. He got past all of us and over to the basket. The scoreboard lit up. Two more points for the Rangers.

After that there was no stopping them. They set us on a full-court chase. Over to their basket. Back to ours. Across again. Back. My lungs felt like I was breathing fire.

A Ranger lunged for the ball just as Zack got it. Zack made a fast aim and the Ranger jabbed him hard with an elbow. The ref's whistle blared. Foul! If Zack got lucky, we'd pick up two points.

Both teams squared off opposite each other as Zack took his place at the foul line. He eyed the basket and dribbled the ball. I said a fast prayer and watched him aim. It seemed like a whole year went by before finally he let go of the ball, but when he did, it made a perfect arc—right through the hoop!

Zack didn't crack a smile. He kept his eye on the basket and dribbled again, his face serious and set. I thought about all the hours we'd spent shooting hoops in my driveway. How my dad had made us a court. How Zack and I had painted the free lightpole we'd gotten from the city for mounting the basket.

Suddenly, an idea burst into my head—an idea *so* amazing, so great, so fantastic, I wanted to shout it out loud! Zack didn't have to go to Chicago for the winter. He could come live with us! Mom and Dad wouldn't mind. It was so simple. Why hadn't I thought of it before?

Zack let go of the ball. It hit the rim, rolled for half a second and went in.

"LET'S GO PINECREST!" the cheerleaders

shouted, clapping, and stomping their feet. "Let's GO!"

Pinecrest claimed the ball and took off. It was like Zack had opened a door, and finally let us into the game. We played harder than we had all morning. Again and again the scoreboard lit up.

With less than a minute left to play we were even, 48–48. My arms hurt from using them to block, but I kept working. Then, all of a sudden, LaMar shot me the ball.

I looked around wildly, my heart thudding. Rangers were everywhere! There was no way I could make a pass with all those flailing arms and moving bodies. It wasn't even safe to try a run for the basket, like I did when we played Silver Maple.

With two seconds left on the clock, I had two choices: stall and let the game go into overtime, or take a shot. I took a wild aim and let it rip.

The ball hit the rim and rolled. Everyone in the field house held their breath as it made a slow, lazy circle along the rim. Once around. Twice. Then, drop! Into the basket it went! The buzzer blared and the crowd roared.

"Mickey, Mickey, you're so fine! You're so fine you blow our minds! Yaaaaaaaay Mickey!"

It took me a second to realize it wasn't just Trish shouting my name this time. It was the entire squad of cheerleaders! We'd won!

"Mick, you did it, buddy! You did it!" Zack screamed pounding me on the back.

The fans poured onto the court. "Spider, you're the *man*!" somebody hollered, offering me a high five. I slapped it and tried to find my parents in the crowd. I couldn't wait to get home and talk to them about Zack's coming to live with us.

Mom was talking to Mrs. Marelli from church. I ran over to her and they both stopped talking and smiled at me.

"Mom, I need to talk to you," I said. I looked at Mrs. Marelli and grinned. "It's kind of important," I explained. She nodded and I turned back to Mom. "If I get dressed now, could we just leave?"

"Of course, honey, but ..."

Before she could finish, Trish ran up, shaking her pompons. "Oh, Mickey," she squealed. "You were awesome out there! Everybody thought so. Brittany said she ..."

"Thanks, Trish," I said, cutting her off. Normally I would love hanging around collecting compliments, but I wanted to get this settled. It was hard not to blurt out my idea to Zack before I even talked to my parents. "I've gotta go," I mumbled, rushing past her toward the locker room.

"I'll be ready in two minutes!" I called to Mom.

"Mickey! Wait a second. I want to talk to you!" It was Coach Duffy.

I glanced over at my mom. She was talking to Mrs. Marelli again. From the looks of things, she was going to keep on talking. Her hands were flying around like she was conducting music. I didn't see either my dad or Meggie, and Zack was talking to some guy who lives on our street.

"Sure," I said following Coach off the court. He walked behind the visitor's scoreboard with me trailing behind. I wondered what the big secret was that he couldn't just talk to me in front of everybody.

I didn't think Coach could be mad at me. If it hadn't been for that last wild toss of mine, Red Oak would be grinning like a bunch of jack-o'-lanterns right now. I sure wished he'd hurry up so I could go.

When we were alone, Coach smiled at me. "Nice work out there, Mickey," he said. "You played hard, and it paid off. I've had my eye on you from the start, you know. You're a little guy in a game where tall is all. But you've got drive, speed, and smarts. Those, along with belief, are powerful things. In fact, you remind me of Earl Boykins. You know about Earl?"

I shook my head no.

"Earl's a short guy too," Coach explained. "He's only five foot five, something like that. He's from right here in Cleveland. After high school he played for Eastern Michigan University. It was only a couple years ago, but I guess you would have been too young to remember." He smiled, like he couldn't believe that was possible.

Coach continued, "Anyway, he helped his school make the NCAA. I'll never forget it. That little guy tore up the court and Eastern ended up beating a powerhouse team—Duke."

"Wow," I said. "They did?" My heart beat a little faster as I imagined myself just like this Earl, tearing up the court in college basketball. If Earl could be a star and Muggsy Bogues, the shortest player in the NBA, could be a star, then maybe I could too. Maybe I really could!

"So," Coach said, crossing his arms over his chest and looking me straight in the eye. "That brings me to why I wanted to talk to you. Zack told me this morning he's going to be moving to Chicago for a while."

My heart pounded so hard I could hear it thumping in my ears.

"Which means I'm going to be needing a new starter. I think you're the guy I'm looking for, Mickey. What do you think? Are you up to giving it a try?"

Oh, wow. Oh, *double* wow! All I could do was nod my head and stand there grinning so wide my face hurt. Wait till everybody heard *this!*

"I'd rather you didn't say anything just yet, though," Coach warned.

So much for climbing on the rooftop and shouting it all over town. But that was OK. I could keep telling it to myself. That wasn't all bad. Sometimes it's cool to have a secret. Especially one as amazing as this. I pulled my mind back to what else Coach Duffy was telling me.

"Zack is doing a fine job for us," he said. "Since he will be here for one more game, possibly two, I don't want him losing spirit. That's why I need you to keep quiet. OK?"

I nodded. The mention of Zack's name wiped the smile off my face like an eraser cleaning math problems off a blackboard.

"Yes, sir," I mumbled. "I won't say a word."

Coach Duffy clapped me on the back and walked away. I felt like I'd just had the wind knocked out of me. Coach had just given me what I wanted more than anything in the world, but he'd also handed me a whopper doozy of a problem. The only way I could make starter was if Zack left. But if Zack came to live with us, he wouldn't be leaving.

"There you are!" a voice called.

I swiveled around to see Mom coming toward me. "I thought you were in such a big hurry," she said when she caught up to me behind the scoreboard. "Dad took Meggie to get candy."

Mom squinted her eyes and looked me over. "What's wrong, Mickey? You look like you've seen a ghost."

"I'm OK," I mumbled. "I'll go get dressed."

"Good!" She glanced at her watch and shoved her arm into the sleeve of her old navy blue coat. "I invited Zack to join us for lunch. I thought I'd make you boys a pizza. Oh!" Her eyebrows shot up as she thought of something. "What was it you wanted to tell me earlier? You seemed awfully excited."

I swallowed hard and looked around. I could see Trish turning cartwheels on the court with Brittany Alberts. Coach Duffy was talking to a couple of dads. Sam Sherman was laughing it up with a bunch of his friends. Zack was heading toward the locker room by himself.

I swallowed hard and couldn't look at Mom. "It was nothing," I muttered. Zack's long, gangly arms and legs disappeared through the doorway.

Mom started to say something, then stopped. "OK then," she said finally. "Let's get a move on it. We've got some celebrating to do!"

I didn't say anything. Suddenly there didn't seem like much to celebrate. But I knew I would. There's no sense wrecking a good pizza.

7

World's Worst
Best Friend

"Hey, Mickey! Good job Saturday!" Justin Sullivan called as I walked into school the Monday after the Red Oak game. He's a fifth grader who has never even talked to me before.

"Thanks!" I yelled back. I tried to sound like it was no big deal to be noticed by an older guy, but my insides were bouncing around like an out-of-bounds ball. If only I weren't still so mixed-up about Zack, life would be perfect.

"Hey, Shrimpo! Wait up!"

I stopped to let Sam Sherman catch up. I hate to admit it, but I actually thought he was going to say something nice to me. He *had* said he was sorry about Zack moving to Chicago. And after all, I *did* win the game for our team.

"Play practice," he barked. "My house. Tonight." He pointed his finger at me and added, "Be there."

That whole "be there" thing was starting to get old. Who did he think he was, a Hollywood producer? We were putting on a fourth grade play, for

Pete's sake. The last I knew, Brad Pitt hadn't tried out for a part.

"Can't," I said, yanking open the door. "If you want to have practice, you need to come to my house. I told my mom I'd start being home more." It wasn't exactly true. What I'd said to Mom was that I'd spend at least one afternoon a week with Meggie. I felt guilty stretching the truth, but I didn't want to go to Sam's house.

Sam shrugged. "Fine. Whatever," he agreed. "I'll bring the script and see you at four."

At 4:00, the whole group gathered around the metal table in my basement. Sam handed us copies of his script. I scanned mine quickly to see what lines Ethan Allen had. There were none on page one. None on page two. None on page three either.

"Hey!" I hollered. "Where are my lines? I don't have any lines!"

Trish frowned. "I don't have very *many* lines," she whined. She took off the baseball cap she always wears and clamped it on her head backwards. That was a sure sign she was getting upset.

"You do too," Sam told her, jabbing at her script with a pencil. "Here. Here. And here."

Trish frowned. "But these lines are stupid," she complained. "I want to say something important, not 'Look what I've made for you, General

Washington.' That's so-oooooo dumb, Sam."

Sam ignored her. "Zack, you're going to play the part of Paul Revere. You get to holler, 'The British are coming! The British are coming!' "

Zack lit up. "Cool," he said. "Yeah, that's good."

I kept looking through the script for my part. Zack had a bunch of lines and Trish had at least a few. Sam had most of them.

Finally, on the very last page I found my part. All I was supposed to do was salute Washington (who, of course, was Sam) and say, "I was glad to win the Battle of Fort Ticonderoga for our country, General. Thank you for making me a colonel. I will try to live up to the honor, sir."

Trish was right. These lines *were* stupid. I started to say so, when a streak of fast-moving fur sped down the basement steps and whizzed by the table. On the way, it snatched the script off my lap and raced into the laundry room.

"Muggsy!" I yelled, jumping up and chasing after my dog. "Bring that back here!"

Muggsy came around from the back of the washing machine with the script in his teeth. I tried to grab it, but he held on tight. I pulled. Muggsy growled. He thought we were playing tug of war. I pulled harder. The script ripped. Muggsy made a sliding turn and ran back out into the other room with his half of the pages hanging out of his mouth.

"Muggsy!" I hollered, running out of the laundry room after him. "What did you do that for?"

But Muggsy was already upstairs.

I handed my part of the torn script to Sam. "Look at that," I said. "My dog doesn't even like your script."

Sam laughed. "Your dog is a mutt," he said. "Nobody would want a dumb little yappy dog like that."

My face burned from the inside out. How dare Sam make fun of my dog! It was bad enough that he made fun of me, but Muggsy didn't deserve it. So what if Sam had a huge Lab, and Muggsy was no bigger than a shoe box? So what if Sam's Lab was as sleek and black as patent leather, and my dog couldn't decide what color to be? My dad likes to say Muggsy was made on Friday with the leftover parts from four other dogs. But, of course, he means that in a nice way.

"I think Muggsy is cute," Trish said loyally. "Don't be so mean, Sam. And change my lines. I want at least one good thing to say. I want to say, 'This flag will be a symbol of our great nation forevermore. Long after we are dead, it will wave on—o'er the land of the free and the home of the brave.' OK? Can I say that? Huh?"

Sam laughed so hard he nearly fell off his chair. "You've gotta be kidding!" he said. "There was no 'land of the free and home of the brave' then. Frances Scott Key didn't write the 'Star-Spangled Banner' until the War of 1812."

Trish crossed her arms. "I don't care," she said. "I want to say it and I'm *going* to say it."

I laughed. "Go for it, Trish," I told her.

"Yeah, go for it," Zack echoed. He grinned at me.

Guilt flooded through me as I grinned back. I looked away. I still hadn't talked to my parents about Zack's coming to live with us. Three times over the weekend I'd tried. But each time I'd remembered that I wouldn't make starter if he stayed. Each time I'd chickened out.

Zack doesn't even know about your idea, a little voice whispered in my head now. *He can't be upset about what he doesn't know.* It cheered me up a little. The big thing right now wasn't Zack anyway, it was Sam and this stupid play.

Meggie clattered downstairs holding something. "Look, Mickey," she said, coming over to the table. She opened her hands and a shower of ragged, white paper pieces fell across the shiny metal surface. "Muggsy did it."

A huge snort of laughter flew out of my mouth. Muggsy had done exactly what I would have liked to have done to Sam's dumb old play.

Trish picked up one of the pieces and looked at it. Then she jumped up out of the chair. "Hah!" she yelled at Sam. "Even Muggsy agrees. He knows you're trying to keep me and Mickey from being bigger stars than you are!"

Sam's face turned pink as bubblegum. "I'm the play writer," he said, standing up too. "The play writer doesn't *have* to listen to the actors."

Trish took off her baseball cap and waved it at him, "They do if they want to *have* actors," she shouted.

Sam sat back down. "All right, all right. You can say whatever lines you want," he said to Trish. "Who cares if they're wrong? I'll just tell Mrs. Clay you made me put them in there."

Sam looked at me and asked, "What about you, Shrimpo? What do you want to say?"

I shrugged. I didn't know what I wanted to say. I wasn't sure what Ethan Allen *should* say.

"All right then, I'll do a rewrite," Sam said, gathering up his stuff. "I'll give you the new pages tomorrow. But I'm warning you, this is the last time I'm changing anything." He grabbed his jacket off the back of the chair and stomped up the stairs, leaving us staring after him.

Trish left a few minutes later to get her bangs trimmed. Zack and I wandered upstairs and flopped on the floor in the living room. Muggsy bounded in from the kitchen and jumped on my chest. First he chewed my hair. Then he chewed Zack's hair. Then he started licking our faces with his rough little tongue.

"Stop! Gross! Stop!" I yelled, laughing. My mouth was open and he'd just licked my teeth. I rolled over and bumped into Zack who was trying to get away too. Five pounds of excited dog was almost too much for both of us to fend off.

"Here, Muggsy! Here, Muggsy!" Meggie called from the kitchen, shaking the bag of dog food.

Muggsy gave us each one last slurpy lick and ran toward his favorite sound. Zack and I lay back against the couch, breathing hard. We were both laughing. I was also scrubbing at my teeth with the bottom of my T-shirt to get the dog germs off.

All of a sudden, Zack sat up straight and let out a howl so awful I jumped a foot.

"Mick!" he cried. "I just thought of something! My dog! What if I can't take Piston to Chicago with me?"

I sat up too. I hadn't even thought about Piston. He was Muggsy's brother and the dog Sam Sherman had stolen from the church parking lot. I'd worked hard to get Piston for Zack. No

way was I going to let anything bad happen to
him now.

"You mean you never asked your dad if he
could go?" I asked, staring at Zack.

Zack shook his head. "Nobody said anything
about him. I guess I just sort of thought he'd be
welcome, but I don't really know for sure. Why
would my aunt and uncle want some strange dog
in their house? It's bad enough they have to take
some strange kid."

I thought about that for a second. Hearing
Zack call himself a strange kid, made me feel sort
of sick, but then I broke into a huge grin. This
was perfect. This was *better* than perfect.

My mom was the one who'd brought Piston
home from the animal shelter in the first place.
She wouldn't want to see him go back there. I
could talk her into letting us dogsit him. She'd say
yes and I wouldn't have to feel guilty about Zack
anymore! I would have done him a huge, big
favor.

"Don't worry," I said to Zack. "Either way,
Piston will be OK. If your aunt and uncle say no,
he can stay here with us until you get back. I'll
talk to my parents as soon as Dad gets home.
OK?"

Zack smiled. "You're the best friend in the
world, Mick," he said.

8

Saving General Washington

"What would you guys think about our keeping Zack's dog for a couple of months?" I asked my parents as soon as we'd said grace. I tried to sound like it wasn't any big deal.

Mom stuck a spoon into the tuna noodle casserole and put a serving on Meggie's plate. "Why would we need to do that?" she asked, carefully leaving out the mushrooms. (Meggie isn't eating mushrooms this week.)

"Yes! Yes!" Meggie cried, jumping up off her chair. "I wanna keep Piston! Please Mama! Pleeeeeeease!"

I picked up the salad dressing bottle and shook it hard. I was glad to have something to do while I explained what had happened with Mr. Zeno's job. I was having a little trouble looking people in the eye.

"Oh, Mickey, that's too bad!" Mom cried when I finished. She let the serving spoon fall against the side of dish and turned to Dad. "Of course we'll take the dog, won't we, Tom?"

"No question about it," Dad said quickly. "Is there anything else we can do to help?"

"Uh … no," I mumbled. "I don't think so. The big thing was Piston." I swallowed hard and poured French dressing over my salad. By the time I stopped, the lettuce was as orange as a pumpkin.

All during dinner, my parents talked about Zack's problem. Mom had baked brownies for dessert, but I didn't stick around to eat any. As soon as I was done with dinner, I asked to be excused.

Upstairs in my room, I flopped down on the bed and stared at the ceiling. Muggsy jumped up beside me and, for once, sat down quietly. He knew I was in no mood to play.

The right thing to do was to ask my parents about Zack. I knew it. Part of me even wanted to do it, but the other part felt like I was already doing a lot to help Zack.

Suddenly an amazing idea flashed across my mind. That was it! If I did a bunch of good stuff for Zack, I wouldn't have to do *this* thing.

Hi, God. Mickey, here. You know how hard I've worked on my game this year, and how much I want to play in the NBA someday. I was thinking. How about if I take really, really, REALLY good care of Piston and write to Zack two times a week and …

I stopped in mid-prayer. God wasn't buying it. I could tell by the sick feeling in my stomach. I rolled over on my side and stared out the window. Somehow there *had* to be a way to work it out so I could be a starter and not have to feel so bad, but I sure didn't know what it could be.

The next morning Sam was waiting for us at school with the new script. "I've got good news and bad news," he announced as he passed out copies. "The good news is, everybody gets more lines." He looked at Trish and grinned. "You even get to say that 'home of the brave' thing," he told her. "But the bad news is, Mrs. Clay wants us to do it tomorrow."

"What? We can't!" Zack squawked. "We don't have time to learn our lines. And we need to practice."

Sam shrugged. "Sorry. If you hadn't made me rewrite, we would have been done. I already told her we'd do it."

"You might have asked us first," I mumbled, plopping down in my seat. I stared at the pages of the script. I now had four lines. Four lines were no big deal though. I could learn them easily.

"Mickey," Zack whispered when everybody went to their seats. "What did your parents say about Piston?"

"They said OK," I whispered back.

Zack flashed me a huge grin. "You're the best, Mick," he said loud enough for everybody to hear.

The next morning, Mom gave me a ride to school so I could carry all the props for the play.

"I'll be at school at two," she promised, as I climbed out of the car. I was loaded down with swords and cardboard muskets. "Meggie wants to see the play."

"OK," I said. "But I don't have a big part or anything."

"That doesn't matter," Mom said. "It'll be fun."

I wasn't so sure I'd call it fun. Especially when I saw Sam Sherman come out of the boys' bathroom in a fancy George Washington costume. He had a white wig, a long coat, shoes with gold buckles, and a shirt with ruffles on the front.

"Where did you get that?" I asked. All of a sudden my horn of plenty gunpowder basket and cardboard musket seemed dumb. Even my dad's real coonskin cap from when he was a kid, looked ratty next to a real costume like Sam's.

"My mother got it at a costume shop," he replied, digging around in a bag. He pulled out the feather pen from Zack's cousin's wedding and frowned. My dad had chopped the ballpoint part off, but he still didn't look happy with it. I ignored him and went over to stand by Trish.

"Look at my neat costume, Mickey!" she said, tugging on the ruffle of her white cap. Usually she tugs on her baseball cap when she talks to me, but there's no way Betsy Ross could wear a baseball cap. "I love it, don't you?"

"You sure have more of a costume than I do," I mumbled. I didn't want to say it, but she looked like Old Mother Hubbard. Her skirt was so long she had to keep hiking it up, which made her shawl fall off. And her cap was so big, the front covered up her eyebrows.

"Ready?" Mrs. Clay asked us, looking around. "Where's Zack?"

"Right here!" Zack called from the doorway. My eyes popped when he walked in wearing a costume almost like Sam's.

"Sam's mom rented it for me," he whispered as we went to take our places in front of the class.

I stood off to the right, clutching my musket. Mom and Meggie were already sitting in the back of the room. But nobody even looked at me. They were too busy looking at Sam and Zack. Even Trish looked better than I did. At least she had a whole costume. I was stuck wearing jeans and sneakers.

Sam went over to Mrs. Clay's desk and pressed a button on the tape player. The sound of "Yankee

Doodle" blared through the room played by a fife and drum. When the last notes faded away, Sam said loudly, "I am General George Washington. The war is over! Freedom has been won!"

He stopped and gave the audience a fierce look. A few girls in the front giggled. "But freedom comes at a price," he warned, ignoring them. He sounded like an announcer on educational TV. "A *high* price."

Leaning on my musket, I wondered why Sam's mom had rented a costume for Zack. Nobody had offered to rent *me* a costume. All of a sudden, the cardboard buckled, and I nearly fell over. I quickly straightened up and smoothed it out, trying to ignore the snickers.

While Sam's voice droned on, I thought about all the times I was left out. The more I thought about them the madder I felt.

"This flag will be a symbol of our great nation forevermore!" Trish was suddenly saying.

I jerked back to attention.

"I was proud to make it, General," she said. Her Mother Hubbard hat slipped down over her eyes. She yanked it back up and scowled at the people who dared to laugh.

"Long after we are gone from this earth, it will fly on in glory," she cried, raising the hoop with the flag in it, high up in the air. She waved them both over her head and shouted, "O'er the land of the free and the home of the brave!" Her Mother Hubbard hat fell down over her eyes again.

The huge flag billowed out behind her like a parachute. But Trish was too busy shoving her hat up to stop it. Slow as a falling leaf, it drifted down—right over Sam Sherman's head! Sam struggled, flailing his arms to get out of the silky cloth. Laughter bounced off the walls like Ping-Pong balls. When his face popped out, his pigtail looked like it was growing out of his left ear.

"That boy is funny, Mama!" Meggie said in a loud whisper.

Sam turned his wig around. "Our g-g-g-g-reat nation," he began. He stopped and looked around the room, his eyes wide. "Our great nation—uh—was built on … uh …"

My mouth dropped open. Sam Sherman had forgotten his lines! He stared at the class, his eyes wild. He looked like he was at the top of a roller coaster hill, waiting to fall.

Suddenly an idea came to me. It was so great it made the idea about taking extra good care of Piston, seem like nothing. I would help Sam Sherman out! Even though he didn't deserve it, I would do it. Then God would be so happy with me, he'd let me off the hook about Zack for sure.

"General Washington," I said loudly. "I understand how you are so—uh—so—uh—upset you can hardly talk. The war was long and bloody, but we—uh ..." I was making up the lines as I went along. "We have a lot to be proud of. Tell us about the midnight ride of Paul Revere."

Sam swallowed hard and looked at me like he couldn't believe it. But he recovered fast. "Thank you, Mr. Allen," he said in his educational TV voice. "I will do that." Then he zoomed right to the part where Zack came in.

After that the play went great. Zack got to ring his bell and holler, "The British are coming! The British are coming!" I got my four lines in. When we were done, the audience clapped so hard Mrs. Clay had to tell them to stop.

A soon as class was over, I grabbed my backpack and the props and went to the car with Mom and Meggie. I asked Zack if he wanted a ride home, but he said no. Sam's mom was giving him a ride, so they could take the costumes back to the shop. I was *so* mad I was almost sorry I'd helped Sam out after all, but all I said was, "OK."

Sam was waiting for Zack by the front door. I didn't even look at him. Now that Zack was leaving, Sam was trying to be his friend.

"Hey, Mickey," he called. (He would never call me Shrimpo in front of Mom.)

"What?" I stopped and turned around.

"Thanks for the help back there."

I nodded and followed Mom to the car. I was so shocked you could have knocked me over with George Washington's feather pen. But that was nothing compared to what came next.

"Mickey," Mom said as we pulled out of the school parking lot. "Dad and I have been talking. We think there might be something else we can do for Zack while his dad is gone. What would you think about him coming to live with us?"

9

Thud! Thud!
The Day's a Dud

"Oh goody!" Meggie shouted from the back seat of the car. "Zack's going to live at our house!"

I didn't say anything.

Mom braked for a school bus and looked over at me. "Mickey?" she asked. "Is something wrong? I thought you'd be happy."

I couldn't answer. My lips felt like they were superglued.

"We don't *have* to do it, if you don't want to," she said, inching the car forward behind the bus. "It's up to you. You're the one who would have to share your room with him. Dad and I just thought it would be easier on Zack, and fun for both of you guys."

Fun? Was she kidding? It would be like having a four-month-long sleep over with the added bonus of two dogs. There was only one thing I could think of that would be any better. The problem was, I had a shot at getting that thing.

"I don't know, Mom," I said, looking out the

window. "I think maybe it's too late. They've got it all planned and everything."

Mom glanced over at me again. "Do you want me to call Zack's dad?"

"NO!" the word shot out of my mouth like an arrow. "I mean, not yet. Let me talk to Zack first."

I stared hard out the window. I knew Mom was watching me with that look she gets when she knows something's not right. But she let it drop, and asked me what I wanted for supper.

"I don't care," I mumbled. Usually I would have hollered, "Spaghetti! Tacos! Chicken and dumplings!" But tonight I didn't care if we had liver and onions. I'd just spotted Zack and Sam climbing into Sam's mom's Jeep. They were too busy talking to notice me. I leaned my head against the window and sighed. Things couldn't get any worse if I worked at it!

The next morning Tony and LaMar were waiting for me at the front door of school.

"Hey, Spiderman!" Tony called as I came up the walk. "Is it true?"

"Is what true?" I didn't have a clue what they were talking about.

Tony clapped me on the shoulder as soon as I came through the door. "You're holding out on us, buddy!" he said. "It's so cool!"

A tiny light flickered in my brain. "Oh, you mean about me being a ball boy at the State game this weekend? You guys already knew that." Ever since this thing with Zack started I'd sort of stopped thinking about being ball boy.

"Not that," LaMar said. "We're talking about you making starter when Zack leaves."

I froze in the doorway. People had to push to get past me. Nobody was supposed to know about that! I'd been so careful not to talk about it. My *parents* didn't even know. Now it had leaked out anyway. I was wrong when I said things couldn't get worse. They had just gotten mega-worse.

"Sam told us last night," Tony explained. He saw the principal coming over to us and whispered, "We'd better keep moving. We're blocking the door."

I trudged after them, my mind whirling. How did Sam Sherman know about me being a starter? If Coach heard any buzz about it, he was going to be mad, and he was going to blame me. I took my science book out of my backpack and stashed the pack in my locker with my jacket. Somehow I had to squash this thing before it squashed me.

"Hi, Mick!" Zack said behind me.

I nearly jumped a foot. I hadn't even thought about how Zack might be feeling about the news—if he even knew.

"Hi," I said. "You scared me. What's up?"

Zack shrugged out of his jacket and hung it in the locker next to mine. "Not much," he said. "I just wanted to tell you I can go Saturday."

My mind went blank.

Zack grinned and tapped his head. "To the State game? You have that free ticket and you asked me to go?"

"Oh, yeah, right. Good," I said. "It'll be fun. So—uh—what else is up?"

Zack shut his locker door and stared at me. "Nothing. Why do you keep asking me that? You're weird today, Mick."

I shrugged and walked into class with him. Zack was right. I *was* weird today. But I could see he didn't have a clue why. I slumped down in my desk and thought about how to keep it that way.

Trish turned around in her seat and smiled at me. "Mickey, that's so neat about you being a starter when Zack leaves," she said. "I can't wait to tell Brittany."

"NO!" I said, louder than I meant to. "You can't tell *anybody*," I whispered. "Who already knows?"

"Just me, Sam, Tony, and LaMar, I think," she said. "Why?"

"Because Coach doesn't want it out until after Zack plays his final game. Do not tell one more person, especially Zack." I whispered. "I mean it, Trish. I could get in trouble."

Trish's eyes widened. "OK, Mickey," she said. "I won't. I promise."

Mrs. Clay was at the front of the room selling lunch tickets. Class was going to start any second. Quickly, I ripped a sheet of paper from my notebook and wrote:

Do NOT tell ANYBODY else about my making starter. Espeshally not Zack. Coach doesn't want him to lose his speerit before the last game. Read this and pass it to LaMar. Mickey.

I underlined Zack's name twice and folded the paper into a tight, little square. Then I wrote Tony's name on the front.

"In your seats please, everyone!" Mrs. Clay called. "We need to get right to work. We'll need extra time this afternoon for those of you who haven't shown your history projects yet."

Everybody groaned. But they sat down and got out their math books. As soon as Mrs. Clay started writing problems on the board I tapped Trish on the shoulder. "Give this to Tony," I whispered when she turned around.

"What is it?" she whispered back.

"What does it look like?" I hissed, handing her the note.

Trish fumbled it like a football. The note

bounced on the desk, made a little arc, and landed on the floor. "I'll get it," she whispered. She leaned over the side of her desk and tried to pick it up. Her arm wasn't long enough to reach. She scrunched down in her seat and tried to get it with her foot.

I watched as the toe of her white sneaker moved back and forth trying to reach the square of paper. She was so close. One more inch. One more …

THUD! Trish slid off the edge of her seat.

Mrs. Clay turned around. The class burst out laughing. I felt like somebody had knocked the air out of my lungs. Trish was sitting on the floor under her desk with the note in her hand. Mrs. Clay could see it plain as anything.

Mrs. Clay frowned. "Perhaps you'd like to share that with us, Patricia," she said in a cold voice as Trish struggled to get up. It was a bad sign. Whenever Mrs. Clay uses your whole name, you're in *big* trouble.

Trish scrambled into her seat, but not before she looked at me. Her eyes were the size of all-day suckers. Mine probably were too. If Trish read that note out loud, I might as well move to Siberia.

I-I can't," Trish said softly. "It's not mine."

Mrs. Clay zoomed right in on me. "Mickey,

does the note belong to you?" she asked. At least she hadn't called me Michael.

I gulped. "Yes, ma'am, but please don't make me read it," I begged. "It has something really, really private in it and ..." My voice trailed off. The inside of a volcano couldn't have been any redder and hotter than my face was at that moment!

Mrs. Clay looked at me and shook her head. "Bring it here, please," she ordered.

I got up and took the note to the front of the class. Thirty pairs of eyes stared at me as I walked all the way up and all the way back to my desk. Mrs. Clay unfolded the paper and began reading. I held my breath and said a fast prayer.

When she was done, she tore the paper in half twice. "You're right, Mickey," she said. "This *is* private. I'm glad you told me that, but you know the rule about notes. I think you need to write a paragraph about why notes are a problem in class."

My breath came out hard and fast. I would write a book if she asked me to. "Yes, ma'am," I said. "I'm sorry." Never had I had such a close call. I hope I never have another one either. It wears you out faster than a full-court press!

At lunch I cornered Tony and LaMar in the hall and told them not to tell anybody about me making starter.

"We already know that," Tony said. "Sam warned us not to. He only knows because Coach works out at the gym with his dad. He said it was a big secret."

"Then why was Trish ready to tell the whole cheerleading squad?" I demanded.

LaMar shook his head. "I don't know. I didn't even know she knew. Sam never told her any …"

Tony interrupted. "I bet she overheard part of it!" he said. "She was standing right behind us waiting for her mom yesterday."

I started to say something about being more careful, when Zack came over to us. The smile on his face was so big it almost connected his ears. "Mick, can I talk to you a minute alone?" he asked.

"Sure," I replied. I told Tony and LaMar I'd see them on the playground, and followed Zack over by the window.

"Guess what?" he said when we were alone. He grinned even wider. "I might get to stay! I might not have to go to Chicago after all!"

My mouth fell open. For two seconds my heart leaped. But then—THUD—it crashed just as hard as Trish had when she fell out of her desk. "Whaaaaat?" I croaked. "I don't get it."

Zack's dark eyes gleamed. "I know!" he said.

"It's so unreal. You aren't going to believe it! Sam Sherman just asked me to move in with him while my dad's gone!"

10

Eight Thumbs Up

I couldn't believe it. Zapped on both counts! I wasn't making starter *and* Zack wasn't moving in with us.

"Are you sure you really want to live at Sam's house?" I asked him. "I mean he hasn't been all that great of a friend." I started to add, "Like I have." But I didn't. No use racking up a lie. God and I both knew what kind of friend I've been.

"I know," Zack agreed. "But it's better now that we're both on the team. If my dad lets me, I'm going to say yes."

I wanted to ask him to come live at our house, but it sounded so lame. He'd know I was only asking because Sam had asked. Anyway, it made me sound jealous. Of course, I *was* jealous, and disappointed, and sad, and mad, and about a million other things.

But there was something else that stopped me too—something hard to admit. I was hoping his dad would say no.

All week I hoped. But every time I asked, Zack

said his dad was still thinking about it. It wasn't until we were in the car on the way to the State game, that he dropped the bomb.

"Guess what? I'm staying at Sam's house for sure," he announced. "Well, *almost* for sure. Dad has to talk to Mr. or Mrs. Sherman first. But they're going to call tomorrow. Isn't that great?"

"Great," I replied weakly. I felt like a popped balloon. "At least we can still hang out."

"Oh yeah," Zack agreed. "Everything will be just like normal."

If Mom heard from the front seat, she didn't let on. She just pointed out some cows to Meggie. All of a sudden I didn't even care about being a ball boy. The worst thing in the world had happened, and I had nobody to blame but myself.

The stadium was huge, much bigger than it looks on TV. As soon as I saw it, the thrill rushed back as strong as a giant wave. I still felt terrible, but the people, music, and noise lit me up like a firecracker.

Dad told the man taking the tickets that I was supposed to be a ball boy. The man checked my name off a list and told a college guy to take me out on the floor. Dad took my jacket and showed me where they would be sitting.

"We'll come down to get you after the game," Mom said. "Have fun, honey."

"Have fun, honey," Meggie echoed.

Zack grinned. "Have fun, honey," he said. It cracked me up.

I could hear him laughing as I followed the college guy. Prickles of excitement zipped up my spine at the sight of the huge shiny court. I was really here! I was at a real live college game! In less than 15 minutes I would be chasing balls for the stars! I shoved Zack out of my mind and decided to enjoy the game. I could feel bad later.

"Hey," the college guy said suddenly, turning around. "Are you Mickey McGhee?"

"I'm supposed to give you something," he said when I nodded. "Wait here."

I stood by the edge of the stands where the announcers sat and looked around. People packed the seats like nibblets of corn crammed in a can, and more kept pouring through the door.

Two boys my age were on the other side of the court tossing baskets. A nervous feeling fluttered in my stomach. I didn't see anybody I knew.

Pretty soon the college kid came back, holding a State T-shirt. "Mike Sherman wants you to have this," he said. "There's a restroom back the way we just came. You can go and put it on there. I'll take the shirt you have on now and give it to your Mom," he offered.

I took the red and gray shirt and broke into a

grin. A note pinned to the front said, "Hey, Spider! Glad you're here! Make me proud, buddy."

I followed the college guy to the restroom and went in by myself. It was crowded, so I tried to hurry. I pulled off my old shirt and unpinned the note from the new one. I couldn't wait to put it on, but there was a tag dangling from the sleeve. I took it over by the sinks where the light was better. Maybe if I was careful I could just tear the tag off.

"No way! Are you kidding? I never even asked my parents," a voice said. I stopped tugging on the tag and froze. The voice was coming from the other side of a short wall at the end of the sinks. I would have known the sound of it anywhere.

"I only told Zack he could move in to make McGhee squirm," it went on. "McGhee knows he won't make starter if Zack stays. He won't want his best friend at my house, so he'll ask him to come to his house. Zack will say yes and that will be that! Bye-bye, starter."

My heart pounded. Blood rushed to my face and my hands started shaking. I couldn't believe my ears!

"But what if McGhee *doesn't* ask Zack to stay at his house?" another voice asked. It belonged to one of Sam's buddies.

Sam laughed. "Oh, he will. That's why I'm not worried. I wouldn't have done it, if I wasn't sure. It wouldn't be fair to Zack. I'm not *that* mean."

Quickly, I yanked off the tag and stuck my head through the neck hole of the shirt. I wanted to get out of there before Sam came around the wall. I hurried out the door, shoving my arms through the sleeves as I went. My heart was banging like a snare drum.

"You OK?" the college kid asked when he saw me.

"I'm fine," I said. "Let's go!" I knew my face was the color of cranberries.

Out on the court I grabbed a ball and pounded it on the floor. Once. Twice. Three times. I started to run, dribbling furiously. How *dare* Sam Sherman do something so mean! I aimed, shot, and scored. I grabbed the ball and aimed again. Another score. He was treating Zack like property in a Monopoly game.

I raced around, dribbling. A kid tried to block me, but I danced past him and scored again. It was so rotten. Rottener than slimy, brown apples. Rottener than month-old eggs. Rottener than potatoes with foot-long eyes.

Slam! The ball smashed against the backboard and through the hoop. Another score.

"Hey, look at that little kid!" a guy hollered

from the stands.

I knew he was talking about me. But I didn't care. I was mad. As mad as Jesus was the time He saw those moneychanger guys in the temple.

Sam Sherman came out on the court, but he went to the other basket. Fine by me. I kept slamming balls and scoring hits. By the time the game started, I was dripping wet and still ready to run.

Mike Sherman led his team out on the court. The fans went wild, screaming and stomping. "Sherman! Sherman! *Sure-Man!*" they screamed. He jogged past me so close I could have reached out and touched him.

"Hey, buddy," he said as he went by. A warm feeling spread through me like fire.

The State team took control of the court. They were giants who could dunk balls with both legs sticking out behind them. I loved watching them do alley-oops. What I wouldn't give to hang off a basket! I was so revved up, I almost think I could have done it, if I'd had the chance!

At halftime, State led by 12 points. The dance squad strutted out onto the court in their sparkly, red costumes and swung into a fast number with a lot of kicks.

"Hey, Shrimpo," Sam said, coming over to stand by me. He mopped his face on the bottom of his shirt. "You're going to be worn out if you keep running that hard. What's with you today?""

Zack was climbing down out of the stands and coming toward us. All it would take is one question—*Why don't you tell Zack what you tried to pull, Sam?*—and Sam Sherman would be busted!

"Hey, guys!" Zack called. "You were awesome! Isn't this cool?"

"It sure is!" I said. All I had to do was ask that one question. One question. "Uh, can I talk to you?" I asked Zack. "Alone?"

"What's up?" Zack asked as we walked away. He turned around and looked back at Sam. "I wanted to ask Sam what time his parents might call tomorrow."

The band was playing my favorite game song, "Hang on Sloopy." My heart felt like it was playing bass. "You can talk to him in a second," I said. "I want to ask you something first."

"OK." Zack stopped by the stands and crossed his arms. "Shoot."

"I know how much you want to go to Sam's," I said carefully. "Who wouldn't, with Mike coming in and out? But I was thinking. You and I always have so much fun and ..."

Zack's eyes widened. "Are you asking me to live at your house, Mick?"

I nodded. "Yeah."

He leaped in the air and let out a whoop. "Oh,

wow!" he shouted. "Oh, *double* wow! I was hoping so bad you'd ask me! But what about Sam?" He stopped smiling and looked over to where Sam was dribbling a ball. "I already told him I'd go to *his* house. It's all set. I don't want to hurt his feelings or anything."

I looked over at Sam too. I knew he was watching us. *Say it. Go on, say it! Tell Zack what you heard*, a little voice whispered in my head. But I couldn't. Zack would be wiped out if he knew Sam didn't really want him to come.

"I know it's all set," I said, picking my words carefully. "But it would be too weird having you over there. Sure, Sam will be disappointed. But you know Sam. He'll get over it."

Zack nodded. "I guess," he agreed. "I'd better go tell him, though. I owe him that much."

I had to swallow hard on that one. "Don't worry. I'll talk to him," I promised. "Look—the game's about to start. Go on back and have fun. I'll take care of everything."

The dance squad moved off the floor, and the ball boys started taking shots again. I ran out, grabbed a ball, and dribbled it over to Sam.

"What was that with you and Zack all about?" he asked, dribbling alongside me.

I took a shot and missed. "Nothing." On the bounce I picked up my ball and aimed it again.

"Oh, by the way," I said real casually, "Zack's going to be staying at my house." I squinted my eyes as the ball sailed through the basket clean as soap.

"Oh yeah?" Sam asked.

"Yeah," I said, scanning the stands for Zack.

A huge smile crept over Sam's face. I could almost see the wheels turning in his head. He thought he'd gotten me. He thought I'd fallen into his trap and invited Zack because I was jealous.

I flashed Zack the thumbs up sign. His grin was wide as he gave it back. So did Meggie, Mom, and Dad. I looked at those eight thumbs in the air and laughed.

"What's so funny?" Sam asked as the State team jogged back out onto the floor.

"Nothing," I replied. Come to think of it though, I should have said, "Everything."

One Extra-Large Miracle to Go

Attention boys!
Basketball Teams Now Forming
Grades 4–6
Have Fun!
Make Friends!
Get Fit!

"Hey, look!" my best friend Zack Zeno shouted, pointing to the sign on the red brick wall of the city pool house. "Just what we've been waiting for!"

I shoved a weird black rock I'd found on the ground into the side pocket of my jeans and went over to check it out.

"Tryouts are Saturday morning," I read. "We're in, buddy!" I slapped him a high five and we pretended to do a jump shot.

Zack and I are total basketball freaks. Someday we're going to be high school hotshots. Then college all-stars. Then NBA pros. We've got it all planned. But until now we figured we'd have to wait until sixth grade to play on a real team.

"Hey!" somebody hollered from the parking lot next to the pool house.

It brought our feet down hard on the sidewalk. Every time I hear that voice I feel like I just got punched in the stomach. I could be at a real live Bull's game and the sound of that know-it-all tone would spoil the whole thing. Michael Jordan could sink a winning three-pointer and I'd be feeling sicker than the winner of a pie-eating contest.

"Hey, Sam!" I hollered back. I always pretend like Sam Sherman doesn't get to me. But it's getting harder and harder to do. Not only does he make my life miserable, but he also gets everything he wants. He even gets everything *I* want, which right now includes a dog and being tall enough to play center.

I know the last one will never happen, but I might actually get a dog someday. At least that's what my mom says. Trouble is, she's been saying it for two years already and "someday" is no closer than it ever was.

"You guys trying out for the team?" Sam asked. He came toward us, dribbling what looked like a brand new basketball. His huge black Lab, Zorro, pranced along beside him sporting a bright red collar.

"We n•ght," Zack said.

"Yeah, we might," I agreed.

Sam dribbled the ball under his leg and lost control of it. It rolled off the sidewalk into the grass.

Zack and I grinned as he ran after it.

Sam picked up the ball and walked the rest of the way to the pool house. "You'd better get in some serious practice then," he warned. "Most of the guys who have a chance to make the team were at basketball camp this summer."

My heart sank. Well, not really. That's just a thing people say when they're upset. But if hearts *could* sink, mine would have ended up somewhere around my ankles. Sam was right. At the end of last year, a player from the local pro team came to our school and passed out flyers about the camp. Everyone who was serious about basketball signed up. Except for Zack and me. Basketball camp cost more than $100. Even without asking, we knew our parents couldn't afford it.

"We don't need basketball camp," I said now, heading toward my bike. "We're naturals."

"Naturals!" Sam scoffed. He laughed so hard he doubled up over the ball. "When's the last time you looked in the mirror, McGhee?" he asked me. "You're a little shrimp."

I picked up my bike from the ground where I'd crashed it and jumped on. Already I could feel my ears burning. It was like Sam Sherman held a remote control. All he had to do was press a button, and I turned as red as a sunburn. I'm the shortest boy in the fourth grade. Most of the *girls* are even taller than I am.

"Size doesn't matter," Zack said loyally, jumping on his bike too. "Mickey's got speed."

I didn't say anything. Sam was showing off his crossover dribble. It was so fast and clean, you could set it to music. He'd sure learned a lot at that basketball camp.

Zorro barked and ran in little circles as the ball bounced across the concrete. Usually I like to watch Zorro, but not today. I rode off toward home with Zack behind me. We didn't talk until we crossed the street and were safely in our own neighborhood. Then he rode up alongside me.

"Don't let him get to you," he said. "We're in. We're in!"

"I know," I agreed. But I wasn't so sure anymore.

At my house, I turned onto the bumpy gravel driveway and Zack followed. Our old ten speeds rattled like two jars of marbles. We squeezed our handbrakes and came to a stop, sending the gravel flying.

"Want to do a little one-on-one before supper?" Zack asked.

"OK." I dropped my bike and got my basketball from the garage. I'd told my mom I'd clean my room after school, but maybe if I didn't go into the house, she'd forget for awhile.

I bounced the ball a few times on the pad by the side door of the house. The thud, thud, thud sound it made slapping against the fresh concrete made my muscles unclench. My dad and I had just poured that pad two weeks ago. We built the frame and everything. When the cement was ready, Dad mounted a metal pole in the ground to hold the basket. Later Zack and I painted it black. Nobody could even tell it used to be a city lightpole we got for free.

I tossed the ball to Zack and he pivoted wildly in all directions, trying to freak me out.

"Dee-fense! Dee-fense!" I shouted, trying to block with my arms.

Zack laughed and shot over my head. The ball hit the rim and bounced off. We both scrambled for it.

"Hi, Mickey!"

I froze, both hands on the ball. There's only one other voice besides Sam Sherman's that can stop me cold, and this was it. I let go of the ball and straightened up.

"Hi, Trish," I said.

Trish Riley lives down the street and sits in front of me in Mrs. Clay's class. It's totally embarrassing to admit this, but she has a monster crush on me. I hate it. Neither Zack nor I want to get involved with girls. At least not until we're 27. Maybe even 30!

She pulled the brim of the baseball cap she always wears down over her forehead and smiled. "You're really good, Mickey. I bet you make the team."

Zack pretended like he was practicing his speed dribble. But I could see his shoulders shaking up and down from laughing. Good? What did Trish Riley know about good? I'd just let Zack complete a throw that should have gone in easy.

"Thanks." I turned back to Zack, but Trish made no move to leave.

"I guess you heard about Sam Sherman," she said.

"What about him?" I could feel my muscles tensing up again.

Now that she had my attention, Trish walked up the driveway. "Last Saturday he landed a pair of baskets in front of 2000 people at an exhibition game."